Shadow and Light

A Novella

SHIRLEY SIATON

SHADOW AND LIGHT
A Novella

Copyright © 2023 Shirley Siaton Parabia

ALL RIGHTS RESERVED.
No part of this book may be reproduced or used in any manner without the prior written permission of the copyright owner, except for the use of brief quotations in a book review. To request permission, contact the publisher at books@inkysword.com.

This is a work of fiction. Names, characters, businesses, events, and incidents are the products of the author's imagination. Any resemblance to actual persons, living or dead, or actual events is purely coincidental.

All brand and product names used in this book are trademarks, registered trademarks, or trade names of their respective owners. Inky Sword Book Publishing is not associated with any product or vendor in this book.

ISBN 978-621-8371-38-5 (paperback)

First Edition, September 2023

Cover by Artscandare Book Design
Interior formatting by Champagne Book Design

Inky Sword Book Publishing
Barangay Quezon, Arevalo, Iloilo City 5000
Republic of the Philippines
inkysword.com

Content Warnings

Warnings for mild profanity, violence, references to murder (including those of minors and men of the cloth), and content of an explicit nature.

Recommended for mature readers 18 years old and above.

Playlist

"The Unforgiven 2"
Metallica

"White Flag"
Dido

"Hold On"
Limp Bizkit

"Building a Mystery"
Sarah McLachlan

"Crash and Burn"
Savage Garden

"Sway"
Bic Runga

"You'll Be Safe Here"
Rivermaya

To the ones who found love in the shadows

The Story

This piece of short fiction, originally dubbed *'Dancing in the Rain,'* was first printed in the literary folio The Accounts: Initial Public Offerings of the University of the Philippines-Visayas, College of Management, Iloilo City.

At the time of its initial publication, *'Dancing in the Rain'* broke the idea of the typical college romance, turning tropes on their head.

After so many years, I wanted to revisit and rewrite it into a novella for my birthday in 2023, to once again capture the unique spectrum of emotions that this story brought to life.

This story speaks of an unconventional, inconvenient love; a love that was never meant to be. And, yet, this love believes that there may even be hope for the most broken of us.

SHADOW AND LIGHT

A NOVELLA

Prologue

The Prized Player

MORNING CAME WITH A HOWLING WIND, THE kind that carried dirt and muck that stuck on the skin and never washed out. It seemed to scream in pain.

Arthur gritted his teeth. The storm, gone as quickly as it had come, was over, but everything in the campus was still drenched from the unforgiving intensity of the downpour.

It would be very cold on the field, not to mention muddy. The football pitch looked more like a swamp when he passed by it on his way to the college's main building.

Coach wanted them to start putting in more hours *now*, before first period, for the next intercollegiate football tournament game. Come rain or flood or any other calamity, they would defend their title all the way up to regionals, for the second year in a row.

He descended the steps to the main building's basement. It was a little past six in the morning. The prized player's first class started at eight and now he was most probably in his lair, practicing those deft knee tricks that brought tears to the eyes of the rival coaches.

As team captain, it was Arthur's job to secure the gear and inform the prized player about that morning's practice not getting cancelled in spite of the field's condition.

Not that he'd care either way, he thought bitterly

The prized player was a tireless machine, not a person. He'd show up, do the drills and rounds, and commit the plays to memory. Arthur often wondered what possessed him to turn down the position of captain, after bringing the team to two regional championships since he was a freshman.

Even as a senior, Arthur was only the distant second choice to lead the team this year. His numbers in goals and successful plays were pathetic compared to the prized player's, as was everyone else's. The man pretty much did not miss goals.

He typed in the door code and stepped inside the basement, which housed a collection of old school furniture and relatively new sports equipment. He knocked on the door of a smaller room inside, once a storage closet for cleaning equipment and a break room for campus cleaning staff, before the lay-offs.

This was now the prized player's residence on campus, because he didn't want to share his space with three other kids in the dormitory next door.

No answer. Arthur turned the knob, finding it unlocked, and pushed warily.

There was nothing in the prized player's room except a sparse wooden cot, an equally drab three-legged table, and a portable clothes rack.

The team helped him load back the equipment only last night, he thought. *Knowing him, he wouldn't move out of this place. It's his lion's den, after all.*

Arthur knew that the prized player had some other stuff around, like dartboards, target posters, and sketches of exotic birds. They were all gone. Nothing was draped on the makeshift clothesline strung across the tiny room.

He stood there and assessed this new information for half a minute.

Arthur took a deep breath and closed the door. He retraced his steps in the basement, retrieving two footballs from the storage racks before he left.

He had better tell Coach that Aragon was gone.

ACT 1

Falling

One

The Dark

I T WAS DARK.

In his world, somehow, it always seemed dark.

He gingerly lowered his body onto a lopsided stone bench overlooking the quad. His muscles ached and his sides burned from the run.

The campus was still cloaked in the night. He had been running for more than an hour, but the sky still resembled a blue-black canopy strewn with thick masses of clouds. Not a ray of sunlight breached his limited view of the horizon; it was still too early for that. The air was thick and heavy, and sullied by city dust.

He felt a detached, perverse satisfaction.

"Aragon?"

A female voice had said his family name. People knew him by that name.

Aragon.

A name full of history. His place of birth was far enough away, but he could still recollect the smells of gunpowder, the crisp click of a gun's hammer, the echo of death cries. They all came with his heritage.

His well-trained eyes made out her silhouette. The lighting in the campus was limited and the few functional lampposts badly needed their bulbs replaced.

"Jeri." Her name fell from his lips. After all this time, he was still surprised at the way he would say it. Softer, slower than his usual speech, and always with awe.

She was dressed in a white top and a denim skirt. The balmy breeze played with the strands of her long, wavy hair. She carried a black backpack, the size of which dwarfed her frame.

He wasn't surprised to feel his chest tighten, his heartbeat accelerate. "What are you doing here? How did you get in the campus?"

He watched her place the bag on the concrete pavement and take a seat beside him.

"I had to see you," she replied simply.

"How did you get in?" he pressed.

He lived on campus, in the main building's basement. He had first lodged in a boarding house, then moved to the dormitory after he'd secured a permanent spot in the college's varsity football team. He was not comfortable with the noise and activity in shared living spaces.

Coach had allowed him to hole up in the old janitors' break room, right next to the storage where the sports teams kept all their equipment. The old man could not refuse the simple request of the college's star athlete and pulled every string he could with Administration to make this strange request happen.

"Being in the Student Council has its benefits." There was a smile in her voice. "I couldn't sleep. I figured you would be here."

"I couldn't sleep, either."

Jeri slid onto the bench next to him. He opened his arms and she snuggled into them. She pressed her face to his chest, not minding his sweat-soaked shirt.

"I really missed you." Her voice was a melodious whisper in the stillness. "It's been so busy with your game and the debates…"

"I missed you, too. A lot."

The confession was a rare display of boldness in terms

of expressing how he felt. This was a first for him, and he did it only for her.

"I wanted to call you earlier, but I knew you'd be sleeping," he went on as he touched her hair, wrapping the smooth strands around his rough palm. The contrast was undeniably appealing. "As always, the best option is to run. Wait it out until the sun finally decides to come up."

She giggled. "You're crazy, Aragon."

He had to smile at her declaration, knowing that the only witnesses were the darkness and her. "Maybe I am, because you're here with me and you're so fucking beautiful."

Her giggles dissolved into a breathless sigh as he leaned in for a kiss. Their lips met tentatively at first, before melding together with a passion that no amount of repetition or familiarity could dull.

As their kiss deepened, he found his hands on her body, his fingers hungrily reaching for the softness and curves under her blouse.

She was in a similar state, her hands pulling at his hair as she pressed her body closer and tighter against his, practically melting into his heated skin.

"Crazy," she repeated, this time in a low growl.

"Come with me," he murmured against her lips. He stood up and took her bag, then held out a hand to her.

Wordlessly and without hesitation, she took it, her eyes wide and luminous in the semi-darkness.

He led her to his living quarters, their own little private sanctuary for more than a year now. When they were together, everything else held little consequence.

In those moments, she was the only one who mattered.

As soon as the locked door shut out the rest of the world, his lips found hers again, gently, but quickly growing more demanding and urgent.

He lost himself in the taste and feel of her, always reminding him of the tart sweetness of apples. It was something he could never get enough of.

For someone who had been taught his entire life not to get too attached to anyone or anything, he knew he had already lost this battle to her, long before he'd ever known what it was he felt for her.

The memory of the first time he saw her was striking in its simplicity and unforgettable in its intensity.

That day remained etched in his memory, the mark it made deeper than any of the arcane teachings that had been repeatedly drilled into him over the years.

From that day on, he knew, somehow, that he'd always belonged to the woman in his arms.

Two

The Dusk

THE ORIENTATION WEEK OF FRESHMAN YEAR at the university dawned cloudy and rainy, perhaps an omen of things to come.

He was a stranger to most of the people around him, more so than usual, even in the boarding house where he stayed. He was surrounded by students from other provinces, but he still stood out like a sore thumb, with his accent and his reputation.

He'd been uprooted from the south, on a full football scholarship. The name Aragon had already made its way all over the country, a football player who had never experienced defeat on the field during his elementary and high school years. The universities had fought over him. He'd chosen this particular one because it was the farthest away.

He left his accommodation very early that day and spent the morning practicing on the field, alone, in the middle of the rain. He had a few hours before the start of orientation; he might as well do something useful. Any kind of training was beneficial.

The rain stopped and the sun broke through the clouds just in time for the freshman events to start. At the college auditorium, he joined the queue of new students quietly, hoping he wouldn't get noticed or singled out.

In sharp contrast to his desire to blend in, Jeri was one of the few brave souls who volunteered to be the freshman batch representative.

He watched her ascend the stage with grace and determination, her gaze sweeping over the crowd before settling on the microphone. Her smile was radiant and genuine. She had thick, dark brown hair that tumbled over her shoulders in waves, framing her round face like a halo.

"Hello, everyone," she began, her voice clear and melodic. "My name is Jerann Castelo, but you can call me Jeri. I'm here today because I believe in a better future for all of us, a future where every student has the opportunity to shine and achieve great things, no matter where each of us came from."

No matter where each of us came from.

He was struck and captivated by her words and the passion behind them.

The rest of her speech rang clearly, sincerely. "What is more important is where we are headed and what we can accomplish along the way. We can do this together if we help and support one another, starting today: right here, right now."

She possessed a magnetism that drew him in, the way her intelligent brown eyes seemed to pierce through his very core, seeing him for what he truly was. She had the gaze of a predator, but it was also warm and welcoming. It was a dangerous, intoxicating combination, one she was probably not even aware of.

It was no wonder she won with a decisive margin; she was a force of nature, a beacon of light.

He thought of her like the sun, a radiant star that burned brightly. It was a stark contrast to the shadows in which he had been trained to dwell, a nameless weapon cloaked in secrecy and anonymity.

Her presence wrapped around him like an embrace. It was a strange, but not unwelcome, sensation, one he got just by looking at a girl who stood and spoke on the podium.

He'd been taught to suppress emotions, to sever all ties to the world around him in order to survive.

Looking at Jeri Castelo challenged all of that.

He mustered the courage to speak with her, to his credit—or perhaps to his doom.

The auditorium was abuzz with excitement as the newly-elected freshman representative descended the stage after the announcements of the college dean.

"Congratulations, Jeri," he said, sidling up to her amid the throngs of students offering their well-wishes. His heart hammered in his chest, unaccustomed to such vulnerability with another person, but her smile eased the tension effortlessly.

"Thank you," she replied. "I appreciate it, uh..?"

"N—" He almost said his name in response, but before he could, a group of adoring girls and boys descended upon her, their voices clamoring for attention.

They'd apparently known her from her high school debate days, and their admiration was palpable in the air that crackled with energy and enthusiasm.

"Hey, Jeri! Remember us?" one of them called out. "We were in the Science High School across the road from you. We had an event on international trade policies."

And just like that, she was swept away by the tide of her admirers, leaving him standing alone in the crowded auditorium.

After that, he always watched her from afar, his gaze

following her as she moved through the campus like a whirlwind. She gave him the regulation blue booklets for their quizzes twice during freshman year, whenever he forgot to buy them—the first time for a History exam, the second for an essay assignment in PE he had to write down fifteen minutes before the class started. He was particularly desperate on both occasions, and she graciously came to his rescue.

Her sunny presence was a constant in his life, shining on him brightly even as he retreated further into the shadows the more people paid attention to him and asked questions about his life before university.

He only ever stepped out of the shadows when it was time to play.

On the football field, he could be exactly as he was, without inhibitions or hesitation. While the ball was in play, he could assert his control, bend his body to his will, outsmart and outrun his opponents.

It was the only time he could let go.

He wished he could let go, too, when it came to what he felt for the girl whose presence he craved almost obsessively.

Sometimes, in the early evenings, he would see her seated alone under the fire tree in the campus quad, the bright blossoms a vibrant contrast to her pensive expression. There was a heaviness in her posture, a burden that seemed to weigh her down as she stared off into the distance, lost in thought.

It was in those moments, when the world around them turned momentarily insignificant, that he saw himself reflected in her eyes.

He wanted to reach out, to bridge the gap between them, but fear held him back—fear of rejection, of inadequacy, of the consequences that came with letting someone in, after so many years of being taught to do the exact opposite.

He did try, one time, at the start of their sophomore year, when she was running for a spot at the University Student Council.

It was dusk, but he knew she was not even halfway done with the day.

She was seated on a stone bench overlooking the quad, as usual, surrounded by a hefty stack of books and the large backpack she carried all over campus. It was a wonder how her petite frame managed to stay upright and even walk around.

It was now or never. He had to take the shot.

Before he could overthink the entire matter of approaching her, he found himself standing next to the bench.

"Hi, Jeri."

He was painfully aware that he cast a shadow over her. Swallowing hard, he stepped out of the way of what little light there was left before the sun completely set.

"Oh, hi." She looked up with a tentative, hesitant smile.

An involuntary shiver ran down his spine as their eyes met. An irrational thought struck him.

Does she know?

He didn't even know what to say. When he thought about it, the only thing he had in common with her was that they were both sophomores—and they had one class together that semester, Philosophy.

He said the only thing that came to mind as he took in the sheer amount of belongings around her. "May I sit with you?"

She made space for him by putting her books in her lap. "Sure. Can I help with you something? Is this about Math 100?"

He took a seat, careful to keep a respectful distance. "Math 100?"

She nodded. "I've been asked a lot lately about tutoring people in Calculus."

"No, not about Math 100, although I would appreciate the help if you've got the time."

Her smile was kind, but he couldn't help but notice

the dark circles under her eyes, the drawn expression on her face despite the genuine light in her gaze.

"I'll have a look at my schedule at the Learning Center, but I'd be happy to slot you in if there are still free spots left."

"Thanks."

Silence fell over them, awkward and heavy.

He didn't know where he got the guts to speak first.

"I just wanted to ask if you're okay. I was passing by and, well, I noticed you've been looking a little…overwhelmed lately."

She studied him intently before saying anything in response. "Am I that transparent?" He wasn't sure if she laughed or sighed. "I guess I didn't realize anyone was paying attention."

"It's hard not to notice when someone's constantly on the move, always pushing themselves to do more."

She looked away, tightening her arms around her books.

He drew back, afraid he had offended her.

"Yeah, well, I've got a lot riding on this year," she finally said, looking back at him with a stiff grin. "I can't afford to slow down."

He doubted the sincerity of her words, but he knew he was in no position to question someone like Jeri

Castelo. He chose not to say anything, shifting slightly in his seat to make a quick getaway before he inflicted any further damage. As he did, his shoulder brushed against hers. Her skin felt warm even through the worn material of his shirt

"I don't look okay, do I, Aragon?"

Her candid, murmured declaration was a surprise. He chose his next words carefully. "You don't have to carry the weight of the world on your shoulders, you know. There will always be someone who's willing to help. You've always helped everyone. It's your turn now."

She looked at him for a long stretch of time before speaking. "You make it sound so easy and straightforward. I guess that's what makes you such a great team player."

He was inexplicably flattered to know that she'd watched him play.

"Thanks."

"You're welcome. I guess I just need to find my balance, with everything that's been going on. It's too late to turn back once I'm committed to something."

"I know what you mean."

She glanced at her watch and sighed. "It's time for me to go. I've got Economics at six."

She made a move to stand up. Before he realized what he was doing, his hand was on her arm.

"Can I help you with those?" He gestured to the hulking backpack and pile of books between them.

Wide-eyed, she nodded. "Sure."

He needed no further prompting or instruction. He slung the bag over his shoulder and relieved her of the books.

"Are you sure it's fine with you? You're not off to practice or anywhere else, are you? I don't want to trouble you, honestly."

He shook his head and, for the first time in what seemed like the longest time, attempted a smile.

"It's okay. Happy to help."

He followed her across the quad and to the classroom.

"Thanks, Aragon," she said as soon as they reached the entrance.

"Anytime." It wasn't lost on him how the other students in the classroom stared.

"I owe you one. I'll let you know if I've still got that free Calculus slot, okay?"

She gave his forearm a squeeze before she turned and made her way into the room. Her touch felt like a white-hot brand on his skin.

"Sure," he replied to her retreating back. "See you around, Jeri."

The erratic pounding of his heart was strange to his ears. Even his breathing pattern had changed, just by being in close proximity to her.

If only you could show me what you really are, he said to her, silently, watching as she joined the others and once more changed into the vivacious girl everyone in the college was familiar with.

If only you could see me for what I really am, too.

If only we could let each other in.

Three

The Distance

His resolve held for a week, at best. After that, he knew he couldn't stay away from her.

Exactly seven days after they spoke on the quad, he found himself waiting outside Jeri's Economics classroom, carefully concealed beneath the shadows of a tree.

As soon as the final bell of the evening rang, she emerged from the classroom, as vibrant as ever, with an entourage of classmates from her political party. They were all laden down with campaign posters, her photograph beaming from all of them.

He wanted to approach her, to talk to her some more

but her companions commanded her full attention. He hesitated, uncomfortable with the idea of others observing their interaction. This was unknown territory to him; the presence of other people made him uneasy. He'd just as soon lose his nerve.

Instead, he opted to wait for her to finish, planning to offer to walk her home. Over the past year, he'd sometimes caught glimpses of her walking on the streets surrounding the university. She probably lived nearby.

He watched her and her team as they dispersed to cover different areas of the college. He chose to remain hidden, waiting for the perfect moment to step out of the shadows.

It was late in the evening when Jeri finally left the campus, laden down with her bag and books. With her head high and shoulders back as if she owned the world, her determined stride carried her towards the residential area. He tried to close the gap between them, hoping that she would see him and maybe even smile in recognition. Something held him back, an invisible barrier he couldn't bring himself to breach.

He knew what it was, at the back of his mind, although his pride would never allow him to speak of it.

Fear.

It was the same feeling he had a week ago, moments before he'd approached her on the quad.

Instead, he followed her from a safe distance, his eyes never leaving her as she approached the less crowded parts of the neighborhood. His thoughts raced, wondering how she would react if she knew he was trailing her like some sort of stalker. He'd been trained to recon and observe unnoticed, and now he used those skills only to see her safely home.

That was it, wasn't it?

To make sure she was safe.

As Jeri walked deeper into the dimly lit streets, his senses heightened. The sound of laughter reached his ears, quickly morphing into something far more sinister. The air grew thick with tension, and his pulse quickened in response.

"Hey there, cutie pie," a gruff voice called out, the words dripping with menace. Four men emerged from the shadows of an alley, surrounding her. "We just want your laptop and your phone, and you can be on your way."

She clutched her belongings to her chest. "Please," she begged, her voice breaking. "I need these for school. I'll give you my money, but please, let me keep my things."

The thugs laughed cruelly at her plight. "You're running for the Student Council, aren't you? You're very famous, even in these parts. You should be able to afford new ones."

His heart twisted; his breath hitched. It wasn't in preparation for the kill. It was something more raw and far less calculating.

It was an overwhelming sense of anger, heavily laced with concern. It drove him to admit that he could no longer remain a passive observer.

He couldn't stay in the shadows now.

She needed him.

It took him a single step to come out into the light, radiating from a nearby streetlamp. "Leave her alone."

The men turned their attention to him, their eyes sizing him up. Beneath their predatory sneers, he could sense their hesitation, an uncertainty in confronting a stranger who dared to stand up to them.

And he wasn't just any stranger.

"Who the fuck do you think you are, college boy?" one of the thugs growled.

"Someone who won't let you hurt her." His tone didn't waver as he felt Jeri's gaze upon him. He counted two knives, one retractable steel baton. The biggest of the men, in all likelihood their leader, didn't display any weapons. The leader probably carried a piece, too, but it didn't matter. They were nothing to him.

"Fine," snarled the biggest man, stepping closer to him with a menacing grin. "We'll just take care of you first."

As the leader lunged towards him, he reacted with barely a thought. His fighting style, as old as time, was subtle, fluid, like water flowing around an obstacle. There was no brute force in his movements, no unnecessary exertion of strength. It was as if he were simply stepping out of their way, guiding their own momentum against them.

"Fuck you!" the leader howled as he crumpled to the ground, clutching at an incapacitated arm. The others stared, momentarily stunned by the ease with which their companion had been defeated.

He didn't give any of them time to recover, or even express their regret at mugging Jeri or challenging him. It took him twelve moves to take the remaining three of them down. It would have taken nine had he wanted to go for the kill.

But she was there, watching him.

In mere moments, all four thugs lay sprawled on the pavement, with fractured bones and egos. They scrambled to their feet, their faces twisted with fear and pain, before fleeing into the shadows.

He stood silently, breathing his way back into a calmer state, before he spoke to her.

"Are you okay, Jeri?"

She nodded wordlessly, still clutching her books tightly to her body. Her eyes were wide, filled with residual fear mixed with gratitude and relief.

"Here. Let me take your things."

She offered no resistance when he moved to relieve her of her backpack and gently pulled the books out of her death grip.

"How...how did you get here?" Her voice was trembling, a far cry from her usual confident manner of speech. "It's so late."

"Football practice ran late. I was just on my way to grab some food when I saw you."

He was relieved when she didn't pry further.

"Thank you," she said quietly, barely above a whisper. "I...I don't know what could have happened if you weren't around. I could have l-lost everything. And I've worked so hard, too…"

Her voice trailed off, as if she'd seemingly stopped herself from saying too much.

"You're welcome." He thought it was the safest, most neutral response. "Do you live nearby? I've seen you walking this way a few times before."

"My grandparents live a couple of blocks away. Most of the time I walk to school." Her voice shook slightly. In the lamplight, he could see the hint of unshed tears in her eyes.

He could easily deal with four armed men, with his bare hands, but not with something like this. He didn't have the training to deal with an oncoming assault of emotions and tears.

He swallowed hard. "Can you walk? I'll take you home. Would that be okay?"

She nodded and, to his surprise, inched closer to him. He could feel her body heat, could see her flushed cheeks.

"Would you like to take my arm?" he offered, not sure why he did. It felt right to say it.

She accepted without hesitation. He didn't mind the weight of her things at all; he was very conscious of how close she was as they slowly made their way through the darkened streets, her hand resting lightly on his forearm. She smelled of something fruity and warm.

"This has never happened to me before," she said softly. "I know this neighborhood and most of the people around. I've lived here since I was seven."

"I'm very sorry this happened to you, Jeri."

"It's fine. It's a good thing you're here."

She stopped walking and let go of his arm when they reached a modest two-story house with yellow wood panels and a red galvanized-iron roof, nestled in a lane of similar-looking houses. "Well, this is me."

He took his phone out of his pocket and gave it to her. "Here. Please put your number in."

She took the phone wordlessly and typed in the digits as requested. As she did, she looked up midway through the task, twice, eyeing him curiously. As their eyes met, something stirred within him—an unfamiliar, yet somehow welcome, emotion.

She handed the phone back and he called her, waiting for her phone to ring. It played a beautifully melodious ballad, crooned by a woman with a haunting voice.

"That's a nice song."

"It's called *'Building a Mystery,'* by Sarah McLachlan," she said, as she took her phone out of her pocket to cut the call. "It's been around for a while, but I really like it."

He glanced at the dimly-lit house before him and back at her. "Promise me you'll call if you ever need anything. I'll be there."

"Really, I don't want to bother you. You've done more than enough and I—"

"Please, Jeri. Promise me." The imploring tone he heard in his voice was surprising even to his own ears.

"Okay. I promise."

A sense of relief coursed through him. He hoped she hadn't said it just to get rid of him.

"I guess I should be on my way."

Before he could react, she put her hand on his shoulder and tiptoed to kiss the lower part of his left cheek, her lips only able to reach as high as his jawline.

He felt like he'd caught fire, the contact leaving a searing heat as if she'd pressed a blowtorch right on the spot where her mouth was mere seconds ago.

"I guess." She took a step back and held out her hands. "Be careful, okay?"

He stared at her uncertainly for several long seconds. *Fuck.*

Was he supposed to hug her now, or maybe kiss her back? Not that he didn't want to. He'd wanted to since he first saw her but…

"My things, please?"

Heat rushed up his neck and suffused his face, making him grateful for the cover of night. Heart pounding, he carefully handed over her backpack and books, hoping she wouldn't see that his hands were actually trembling.

"There you go. Good night, Jeri."

"Good night."

With a nod, he turned away from her and began to retrace his steps to the campus. In truth, he still hadn't eaten anything since lunch, but now—

"Nick?"

Her voice carried quietly down the empty street.

Nick.

His first name was Nicholas, but none of his peers ever called him by it. Only the teachers who called the roll ever did.

He was Aragon to people in the university and this city.

She didn't even use his complete given name. Just Nick, as if she'd known him all her life.

He looked over his shoulder to see her still standing in front of the house, looking at him dead on.

"What is it?"

"Thank you. I'll never forget this."

He turned to face her, pushing his hands into his pockets to prevent them from doing something stupid—like close the distance between them again and take her in his arms.

He hesitated before launching into the question he'd really wanted to ask. "Can you do me a favor then?"

"Anything."

"Can we keep this between us? I don't want people to make a fuss."

"I understand. You can trust me."

He nodded. "Thanks, Jeri. I'll see you tomorrow."

"See you tomorrow, Nick."

His walk back to the campus was a blur, the idea of

dinner losing its appeal the more he thought of what had just happened.

The fight, if one could even call it that.

The first time he'd shown an outsider even just a tiny glimpse of the true extent of his abilities.

The kiss.

The first time a girl had put her lips anywhere near him.

The promise.

The first time he had willingly offered his protection to someone without a price.

The name.

Nick. Spoken as if it were the most normal thing in the world for her to do.

He didn't realize he was already within the university's walls. He pulled out his phone, holding on to it tightly, as if it was tethered to the girl who was now hopefully safe and secure blocks away.

He took a deep breath and dialed her number. As he listened to the ringing sound, he felt tight knots form in his stomach, only to loosen when he finally heard her pick up at the other end.

"Hello, Nick?" she answered hesitantly.

"Hey, I'm sorry to bother you. I just wanted to check on you."

"Thank you," she breathed. "I'm…I'm fine. Just a little

shaken, that's all. But I should be okay. I'm just getting ready for bed. What about you? Did you get any dinner?"

"Ah, it's fine," he replied, glancing at the deserted quad around him. "I'll be off to the gym soon."

"Really?" she sounded incredulous. "Do you ever sleep at all?"

He didn't answer, evading the question with a subtle deflection. "I'm just glad you're okay, Jeri."

"Well, I owe you one. I'll bring something nice for you to eat tomorrow to make it up to you. I'm so sorry you missed dinner."

"Please, don't worry about it," he insisted, uncomfortable at the thought of someone going out of their way for him.

They spoke briefly about her campaign, and he couldn't help but admit that he would vote only for her, despite there being two available spots on the University Student Council.

"Your support means a lot." Her voice was now lighter, less tense. The more relaxed she sounded, the better he felt, too. "But I have to say, it's because of you that our university is back on the sporting map. It's like you've proven to the entire region that we're not just a bunch of nerds with our noses buried in books."

As their conversation continued, she asked about his

well-being, if he needed anything or if there was any way she could help him, so far from home. The genuine concern in her voice moved him, and he understood why she was so beloved by everyone at school.

As they spoke, he walked to the bench on the quad where Jeri usually sat and assumed her place under the shelter of the tree. When they finally exchanged goodbyes and he waited for her to cut the call first, he realized it was barely an hour before midnight.

He stared down at his phone as if it could provide answers to the swirling questions in his mind.

What did he really feel for her?

Did she have any idea about it? What would she think of him if she knew?

What was he going to do about any of it, as someone living on borrowed time?

The stillness of the night wrapped around him heavily. Most students would have been fast asleep by now, but sleep rarely came easy to him.

As he entered the dimly lit gym adjacent to the auditorium, he took a deep breath, inhaling the familiar scent of sweat and rusted steel that permeated the air. This was his sanctuary, a place where he could lose himself in his training and forget, if only for a little while, the real weight of his dual existence.

With each precise strike against the punching bag, each rep of the heavy barbells only he could lift, he tried to push all thought out of his mind, focusing only on the screaming of his muscles.

But thoughts of her persisted, even as he tried to punch and kick harder than usual, lift heavier than he normally would.

He paused in his training, pressing his face to the cold and grimy wall, trying to ignore the hunger that raged in his stomach.

"Damn it," he muttered under his breath, slamming his fist against the wall in frustration. The pain that lanced through his hand was a welcome distraction.

He needed not to think about time, about how he couldn't take it back no matter how strong he became, how hard he trained, or how much determination he possessed.

Time was his greatest enemy. He had already used up more than a year of it; he had less than three left.

Three years was nothing. It would all flash by in a heartbeat, and he would be dead again.

He was fighting a losing battle.

But he wasn't going down easily.

Four

The Divide

He found out they were both creatures of habit.

That small snippet of realization took down one more piece of the wall around him, as he unknowingly began to let her in.

The day after he'd walked her home for the first time, Jeri brought him a meticulously packed bundle of food: steamed rice, small cuts of grilled meat, and a piece of fruit. She turned up at the corner of the field right after the team's morning practice session. She repeated this the following day, this time with a small container of stir-fried noodles and vegetables clutched in her hands.

She became his tutor in Calculus, too, in twice-weekly sessions they spent in a corner desk just outside the library. Away from the confines of the Learning Center and the strict silence of the stacks, the spot always seemed reserved for her. Once he'd asked her if she'd signed him up officially as a tutee; she'd just shrugged and smiled.

He became, unofficially, her shadow. He walked her home almost every day, especially on those times when she stayed on campus until late in the evening. Even on days when football practice was supposed to drain him of energy, he found himself accompanying her on the darkened streets, seeing her safely to the yellow house with the red roof, which always seemed devoid of life.

As the days flew by, they became part of each other's daily routines.

Shortly before the University Student Council elections, he picked her up from her Economics class. They were once again subjected to curious stares, this time a little more openly. He wondered how she could live with such scrutiny every day.

"Hi." Jeri appeared at the doorway of the classroom, greeting him with a small smile.

"Ready for some Calculus?" He extended a hand, knowing she understood what he meant.

She turned over her backpack without question.

"Always. Let's get you ready for a great score during the mid-terms. That way you won't have to stress so much on the finals."

They walked across the quad to their usual spot outside the library. As the night deepened, they delved into derivatives and integrals, her patience with him as saintly as her presence was soothing.

They were packing up their things when she hesitated before leaving the library building.

"I've been meaning to tell you," she said hesitantly, stopping on top of the steps that led to the quad outside. "I didn't want to talk about it before, but I thought you should know."

"What is it?"

Were people talking about him, to her? What did they know?

She averted her eyes from his before speaking, clutching her books to her chest and belly. This was her self-preservation reflex, using her books to protect her vital organs.

It was strangely endearing.

"Ever since we started spending time together, my campaign has picked up. People are taking notice, especially the sororities. I've gotten two invitations to pledge in the past week. They thought, well, that I'm your girlfriend."

She swallowed hard and looked him in the eye. "I'm so sorry."

"Why?" He held on to her gaze as he relieved her of the books. She need not worry about anything hurting her, as long as he was around.

"Why what?"

"Why are you sorry, Jeri?"

She bit her lip and shook her head. "I don't know. For people misinterpreting our friendship, I guess. I just don't want you to think I'm using you or anything."

"Using me?"

"You're practically a celebrity in this school, Nick. Anyone close to you would have a higher clout than they'd ever have on their own. That includes me."

Had he been someone else, he would have laughed at the ridiculousness of the idea. But he could sense her anxiety, her fear of being misunderstood.

He didn't know the first thing about politics, but fear was something he understood intimately.

"How can you use me, when I'm doing all of this by choice?"

"Are you really?"

He nodded.

He wasn't even finished with his response before he

found himself, laden down with her backpack and her books, in her arms.

She was hugging him. It was awkward and lopsided, but he didn't care.

"I don't care what people think," he said, uncertain on how to respond using his actions. He couldn't even move that much.

She gave him a squeeze before letting go. "Thanks. You're a really great guy, you know."

He felt a mixture of relief and loss once she broke contact. "Alright. Okay, let's get going."

The walk to her house was quiet and leisurely, with a few snippets of conversation in between; they talked about the start of the intercollegiate sports season, about the upcoming elections.

Life, for a while, was simple.

When they reached her house, Jeri hesitated at the gate as he handed over her things. She went on tiptoe as before. This time, he bent down so she could reach his cheek properly.

"That's better," she murmured against his skin before kissing him. "Thanks, Nick."

As soon as the books were in her grip, it was his turn to put his arms around her.

For the first time in his life, he hugged a girl.

He could feel the slight tremble in her body. She was wonderfully soft and warm to the touch.

"Good night, Jeri."

With her hands occupied, she leaned into him, her face nestling against the crook of his neck. "Good night. See you tomorrow."

As he walked away, the distance between them growing wider with each step, he felt the familiar buzz of his phone in his pocket.

Barely a moment had passed since their goodbye, and already she had sent him a message.

Thanks for your kindness

You're the best

He was about to text her back when the world around him shifted, a sudden chill creeping up his spine.

He was no longer alone.

Eight shadows materialized around him, some of their faces familiar. Half of them were part of the same group of men who had mugged Jeri weeks back.

This time, however, three of them brandished guns. The metal shone dully under the dim glow of the streetlights.

"Go back to whichever hell you came from, hero."

He recognized the leader, feeling a sudden pang of

sympathy for him. If the would-be gangster thought he could save face, he was in for another disappointment.

An icy calm settled over him as he assessed the situation, his mind racing with possible strategies and outcomes like a high-speed game of chess.

He stared at the barrel of the gun closest to him. His voice was steady when he spoke. "Over my dead body."

The men laughed, their jeers echoing through the empty streets.

"If you think the tricks you used to impress your little girlfriend would work on us, you're fucking wrong, kid."

"Those tricks worked very well the first time. I can still remember how quickly you hit the ground."

"You're such a smartass, aren't you, college boy?"

"Just telling the truth." His jaw clenched as he inhaled deeply, drawing on his years of training to center himself before a fight.

He knew he shouldn't be doing this. He'd traveled so far to get away from it all, and yet here he was, letting himself get dragged right back into a world of violence. It was a vicious circle, one he couldn't seem to escape.

The fight broke out with a sudden ferocity, but he saw everything unfold in painfully slow motion. His fists connected with jaws and torsos, bones shattering under the force of his blows. He wove through the group of men, ducking beneath wild punches and countering with devastating precision. It was almost as if he had never left, the muscle memory of countless sparring sessions and battles awakening within him.

The fight raged on outside, but inside him settled a numbing realization. As he sidestepped and countered attacks around him, he accepted the inescapable truth: a normal life was never truly meant for him.

He was, after all, Cain.

Twin to death, forged in blood.

As he battled the men, dodged their knives and bullets with an almost insulting ease, he understood that as long as he lingered in the shadows, violence would continue to claw at him, always demanding to be acknowledged.

And so he lunged forward, disarming two of the men of their guns in one fluid, practiced motion. The cold weight of the weapons settled into his palms, feeling both alien and familiar all at once. They were imitation guns; cheap, soldered versions of the perfectly balanced Glocks he usually favored.

Fake gun or not, it would be so easy to pull the trigger, as natural to him as breathing. For a brief moment, he considered it.

Instead of aiming for the sweet spot between their eyes, as he had been trained to do, he shifted his aim, targeting the knees of the men before him. The gunshots rang out like muffled thunder, encrusted in rusty shells.

"Stay away from me and the girl." He stared down the last man standing, who still clutched his imitation gun with trembling hands.

"Or what?" the man challenged, a desperate defiance in his eyes.

Without hesitation, he fired again, the bullet tearing through the gunman's fingers, wrenching the weapon from his grip. Blood splattered on the grimy, trash-littered pavement as he turned away, as quickly as he had finished the fight.

He knew he had to move fast. Someone would have heard the shots, no matter how late in the night it was. Someone would investigate. It was only a matter of time.

With a heavy sigh, he bent down and collected the weapons of the fallen men, their moans and curses a grim soundtrack to his calculated actions. He found one of them wearing a fairly large jacket; he kicked the man over and ripped the jacket off him, using the fabric as a makeshift bundle for the guns and blades he'd gathered.

Moving with laser focus, he found an empty alley a few blocks away, just around the corner from the university. He entered the darkened area cautiously, ensuring he was alone before getting to work.

He didn't need light to guide his hands as he disassembled the fake guns and broke the blades off the knives' hilts. Using his powerful left leg, he kicked open a nearby manhole, the metallic clang setting his teeth on edge.

One by one, he dropped the pieces of his handiwork into the drainage, watching as they disappeared into the murky sewage below. The darkness swallowed the remnants of his violent encounter.

He was the only one who remained, aside from the eight men and their broken bodies. If they wanted a third round, he would gladly give it to them. This time, none of them would be walking away.

As he made his way back towards the university, the distant sound of police sirens pierced the night air.

His reaction to the sound was a first: his heart pounded in his chest, mingling with a rush of adrenaline and fear through his veins. In the past, he wouldn't have cared about the consequences—escaping and disappearing into the shadows would have been second nature to him.

But, now, things had changed.

Jeri.

With her long brown hair and equally dark eyes, with her smile and sweet little kisses. She'd hugged him earlier, hadn't she?

She'd brought him food every day, too, yet another burden for her to carry.

A random thought crossed his mind as he made his way through the darkened quad, his gaze brushing past the bench where she usually sat in the late afternoons.

More than half the books she always carried were not for her. They were for the people she tutored, including him.

The thought of being apart from her caused him physical pain, a gnawing sensation that ate its way from inside his chest.

He couldn't leave now.

He couldn't ever leave her.

Upon reaching his room, he sank onto the bed, his heart still racing. No amount of breathing techniques seemed to work in calming it down.

He knew there was only one way to deal with it.

He picked up his phone with trembling hands, skinned and bloodied from the fight, and dialed her number.

She picked up after four rings, her voice groggy when she answered. "Hello, Nick?"

"Hi, Jeri," he said softly. "I'm back on campus."

Something about his response must have sounded off to her. Her next words were more alert. "Are you okay? Have you eaten anything?"

The answer to both was a resounding no, but he didn't have to tell her. He hesitated for a moment, then forced a smile into his voice. "Yeah, I'm fine. I just wanted to say good night."

"Are you sure you're okay? Why don't you have some of those sandwiches I brought earlier? You haven't eaten them all yet, have you?"

The white plastic container with the green cover was on the tiny table next to him, already empty. Ever since she'd started bringing him food, he would wash those pieces of Tupperware religiously and returned them to her, squeaky clean and spotless, the following day.

"I have a few pieces left, thanks." He hoped the lightness he affected in his tone was enough not to make her any more concerned. "You're a lifesaver."

"I'll get some more food to you in the morning, okay? I'm so sorry our session ran late. Next time you don't have to worry about walking me home. Everyone at school will kill me if anything happens to you. Your coach will probably string me up on the flagpole."

"Nothing like that's going to happen," he assured her, cringing as the sterile fluorescent lights illuminated the torn, uneven skin on his knuckles. He'd have to make up some excuse about the punching bag ripping, then he'd have to rip the real thing convincingly. "I'm perfectly fine. I just wanted to say good night."

"Um…Nick?"

"Yeah?"

"Promise me you'll let me take care of you. You're so far from home and you're always doing something the rest of us can only dream about."

He didn't answer. He stared at the phone, as if she was speaking in a foreign language he didn't understand.

"Hello?"

"I'm here."

I'll always be here.

He desperately wanted to tell her how he really felt.

He was scared and lonely, hungry for her touch just as much as his body craved sustenance. He was hurting inside and out, his limbs reeling from the exertions of his grueling training routine on and off the field, from the fight he could have easily ended with well-placed gunshots.

Most of all, he really wanted to be with her.

If only for a short while.

"You promise, right?"

"Right."

She paused. He thought perhaps she wasn't satisfied with his answer. She was, after all, a very intelligent person. It would only be a matter of time before she saw right through his lies.

He was relieved when she finally said something. "You sure you're okay?"

"Yeah. I'm fine, Jeri. Good night. I'll see you tomorrow."

"Good night, Nick. See you tomorrow."

She was gone, the line cutting to static, then to the cold dial tone of the mobile network.

He could only stare as the screen blacked out and locked, just like him.

His existence was blacked out and locked from the rest of the world

He lay on his tiny bed, clutching the phone to his chest, allowing an exhausted sleep to slowly claim him.

But it didn't take too long before he woke up, shaky and disoriented, because there really was no escape from the shadows, where he belonged.

Five

The Dance

It was a fateful Friday when everything changed

Anticipation hung heavy in the air as the balmy October day slowly gave way to a cool afternoon. He adjusted his red jersey one more time, unable to deny the real weight the Number 4 held for him.

Today was the day. Their first football game of the intercollegiate sports season and Jeri's fateful election for the University Student Council. He took a deep breath and glanced at the clock. It was time to meet his team for the pre-game prep and warm-up. They were last year's regional champions; the expectations this year were quite high.

As he left his room, a cacophony of voices and laughter filled his ears, but his eyes were drawn to one particular sight. There she was, waiting for him just outside the building.

"Hey, how are the elections going?" He closed the distance between them, still unable to understand how she could still think of him with everything else she was doing.

"I...I don't know yet," she stammered, clutching a Tupperware container tightly in her hands. "But I wanted to give you this. I'm sorry I didn't see you this morning. My party-mates and I had to be at the polls extra early to say hello and thank the voters." She hesitated before finally revealing the container's contents: spaghetti.

"Thank you." He took the Tupperware from her hands, noticing how they trembled. It just wasn't her hands. She was pale and her entire body was shaking.

Gently, he took her things and guided her to a nearby bench. "Sit down. You look like you need a minute."

As soon as they were seated, her eyes met his, and she began to cry. The sight of her tears tugged at something inside him, an ache that seemed to mirror her own pain. He wanted to reach out and comfort her, but the words caught in his throat, uncertain what to do with someone in tears. He could kill the cause of her pain, but that wouldn't really help in the long run.

"Do you…do you want to talk about it? Did someone hurt you, or say anything bad?"

Much to his relief, she shook her head. At least that was one less thing he had to worry about.

As her tears flowed, he hesitated for a moment before pulling her into an embrace. Without their usual barriers of bags and books, the sensation of holding her was new yet somewhat familiar; it was as if his arms were designed to cradle her smaller form. Despite her obvious distress, it felt good to hold her.

"Oh, god," she muttered. "You've got a game and here I am ruining you day."

"Don't worry," he said softly, trying to sound as reassuring as possible. "Just tell me what's wrong."

She sniffled, wiping away the tears that stained her cheeks. Her eyes darted around for a moment before they settled on his face.

"I'm scared, Nick. I'm scared shitless of losing, of failing, of being told I'm not good enough. I feel like I have no value if I don't do something meaningful with my life."

The raw honesty of her words cut through him, and he realized just how much pressure she had been under during this entire campaign. He thought back to all the times he had struggled with his own feelings of inadequacy, with the pressure that he had to be stronger, faster, better than everyone else.

"You mean a lot to so many people, Jeri. You don't have to prove your worth to anyone."

She shook her head, her eyes filling with fresh tears. "I feel like I only have value when people need something from me. That's why I tutor and help others. I want to show everyone that I'm not just...disposable."

Somehow, he felt offended on her behalf. "You're not disposable at all. How could you be, when you mean everything to me?"

Her eyes widened in surprise as his words sunk in, and for a moment, she seemed at a loss for a response. When she finally spoke, her voice trembled with uncertainty.

"Y-you mean you—"

"Yes," he interrupted, pulling her close again, this time without hesitation and awkwardness. "I mean it."

Her arms went around him as her tears soaked into the fabric of his jersey. "You're the only one who really understands, you know. It seems you always know why I need to do what I'm doing. You never question or doubt me. Lexie does, she thinks I'm trying too hard. She worries about me, but I think she's scared of how far and how hard I push myself sometimes. She thinks I might end up hurting myself"

"No," he said firmly. "While I'm here, I won't let that happen."

He knew her best friend tried to understand her, but even Lexie couldn't see past Jeri's relentless drive to succeed. He understood Jeri's need to prove herself, better than anyone else. He'd known it from the start, deep down, the first time he'd seen her speak at the podium during freshman orientation.

"I'll always try to help without asking for anything in return or judging you. Just tell me what to do. I'm yours to command."

Her eyes shimmered with unshed tears as she drew back to look at him. "Why are you so wonderful?"

"It's because of you, Jeri. I don't know what I'm doing half the time, but being with you just feels right. Everything falls into place, as if we're meant to be."

"Meant to be?" she echoed, her eyes searching his. "You mean...together?"

"I don't know," he admitted, shrugging slightly, "but it sure feels that way."

With that, she dove back into his arms. He held on to her quietly for several minutes, memorizing her breathing pattern, the heat of her body against his, and the warm, fruity scent of her skin and hair.

Leaning down, he dared to press a kiss to her forehead.

"Let's have dinner together tonight. We can talk more then. I've got my stipend, so we can afford a full spread at one of the eateries across the road."

She giggled through the remainder of her tears, her hands warm as she squeezed his cheeks gratefully. "If I win, it will be my treat, but there's the annual mixer party tonight, remember? If you're coming, we'll see each other there. But make sure you eat first, okay?"

"Sounds perfect," he agreed, taking the container of spaghetti she had prepared for him. "Will you be at my game?"

"Front row," she promised, hugging him quickly before she jumped back to her feet. "Cheering the loudest for you."

He watched her walk away and gave her a wave before she disappeared around the corner of the main building. He crossed the quad and made his way to the classroom next to the field where his team had gathered to prepare for the big game.

The buzz of excitement and tension filled the room. His teammates immediately noticed the Tupperware Jeri had prepared for him, now a familiar sight; their teasing was good-natured and light-hearted.

"Hey Aragon, we're jealous," remarked a senior. "You've got a sweet girlfriend who's probably going to win the election, too. How does it feel to be The Man?"

A freshman chimed in, too, shyly, his eyes wide with admiration. "You've got everything, don't you, Aragon? We can only wish to have half of what you've got."

Before he could respond, their coach walked in, tablet in hand, and began outlining plays and strategies for the game against the maritime college down the road. They were rumored to have strong players this season, but some of those players carried an arrogance from being high school superstars.

After the meeting, they moved to the field to warm up with stretches and team drills. Before he put his phone away next to the makeshift bench at the end of the field, he gave Jeri a quick call to check if the results of the elections had been announced.

Her voice was still shaky from the earlier tension but much calmer. "No, not yet. One of my poll watchers told me I was leading the count about fifteen minutes ago. I'm sure the counting will be over by the time your game finishes."

"Can't wait." He could feel his chest expand, as if there was a balloon of emotion inside him. "Good luck."

"Thanks. Good luck to you, too." She hesitated, then added, "I'll be on the bleachers watching you play. I just wanted to say…" Her voice trailed off, and he heard her take a deep breath. "Never mind. I'll see you later."

"See you." He wanted to know what it was she was trying to say, but now wasn't the time. He put his phone away and joined his teammates on the field, his eyes scanning the bleachers for her face as the number of spectators grew.

The game started shortly, the roar of the crowd filling the campus as he took his position on the field.

He surveyed the opposing team. To their credit, it was a formidable, meticulously assembled line-up, far better than last year's. They had taller, bulkier players; it was an obvious attempt to stuff the roster with people who were physically strong and had a longer reach, similar to him.

As the first half of the game unfolded, he found himself relentlessly pursued by the opposing team's defenders. He could sense their frustration growing with every missed opportunity to stop him. They could fill their ranks however they chose, but they would always have to contend with his real training.

With a few minutes left in the first half, he saw his chance. The ball landed at his feet in a deftly executed pass from his team's vice-captain.

He wove through the opposition like a shadow slipping through cracks of light, the ball seemingly under his complete thrall. Time seemed to slow as he closed in on the goal, his focus narrowing until all he could see was the steel contraption and the grimy white net it held. He planted one foot, drew back the other, and unleashed a strike that sent the ball hurtling into the net.

Goal.

The crowd erupted into deafening cheers that shook the ground. As he jogged past the bleachers, his eyes locked onto Jeri's face amid the sea of spectators. In that moment, it was as if they were the only two people in the world. He waved to her and she waved back, her face splitting into a bright smile.

The second half of the game proved even more intense than the first. The opposing team held nothing back, their defenders swarming around him with more deliberate attempts to keep him away from the goal. They tried to injure him, several times, but he deftly evaded their attacks, as simple as countering deadlier assaults with firearms and blades.

He could feel Jeri's eyes on him, as sure as he could remember her asking if he thought they were meant to be together. As he took position for what could be the decisive goal, he thought of his real answer, and with a surge of determination, he launched the ball towards the right of the net, just a few inches out of the goalie's reach.

No one could stop him.

It was a goal.

The bleachers exploded in wild celebration. He was

surrounded by his teammates, coaches, teachers, and classmates, all of them caught up in the euphoria of victory.

The roar in the field had barely subsided when another round of cheers broke out, this time originating from somewhere near the school auditorium.

"Castelo won!" someone shouted, their voice carrying above the din. "She got the most votes out of all the candidates!"

It seemed that today was a day of victories for both of them. Excusing himself from the merriment, he stepped away from the throng of people and retrieved his phone from the bench to call her. To his disappointment, she didn't pick up. Perhaps she was already caught up in her own celebrations.

In the aftermath of the game, the team gathered for an enthusiastic debrief, discussing their plans for winning the regionals once more and defending their title. After the meeting concluded, he retreated to his room, his phone still clutched tightly in his hand. He hesitated, wondering if he should call her again. He didn't want to impose on her well-deserved victory.

Before he could decide what to do next, his phone rang, displaying the name and number of the team's vice-captain, Arthur Posada.

"Hey, Posada."

"Hey, just calling to remind you to come to the college's mixer party tonight, Aragon. It's important we show our solidarity, and the administration will be there. You know how they like to see scholars putting in an appearance. Besides, they all want to see you."

He'd already decided to attend the party, but a reminder of his obligations to keep up appearances was the reality check he needed. He thanked the vice-captain and got ready for the night, dressing in his cleanest, newest blue polo shirt and jeans.

The college mixer was already in full swing at the auditorium by the time he arrived, feeling slightly out of place amid groups of chattering students and loud, thumping music. He wasn't one for social events and tried to avoid them as much as he could.

As he joined his teammates, he was met by an approving nod from his coach and the warm smile of the college dean.

"Congratulations, Aragon," the dean said, shaking his hand firmly. "You've earned that scholarship. Everyone here is proud of your achievements for the university."

"Thank you, sir. It's my honor."

"How is your family taking this? With you so far away but doing such great things for our school?" The look on the dean's face was equal parts sympathy and understanding.

"They are very proud, sir. My brothers can't wait to see me again so we can train together."

"That sounds like good fun," said the dean, clapping him on the back. "Enjoy tonight's party, Aragon. My old bones can only stay until ten, but you kids have fun the rest of the night. Make sure to keep it clean. We don't want the police digging around in the morning."

The dean excused himself and made his way to a group of teachers across the room.

He glanced over at his teammates, who were already enjoying food and soft drinks from the catering tables. He watched as a group of girls and other admirers descended upon them, asking the players to dance or engage in conversation.

Never comfortable with such attention, he quietly backed away from the crowd and, as always, inched into the shadows.

He surveyed the sea of people before him, as the flashing lights installed around the auditorium dipped and swung about in time with the music.

Where was she?

He was so caught up in his thoughts he never noticed the person who walked up to him and tapped his shoulder lightly. He turned around to see Jeri standing before him, her eyes bright, her cheeks flushed even in the dim light.

"Hey, Aragon," she said playfully, yet her voice wavered ever so slightly. "If you don't dance with me, I will kill you."

His breath caught in his throat at her words, surprised by the uncharacteristic boldness in them and the sudden rush of desire he felt towards her.

She had on a dress with green and white stripes that brought out the smoothness and pinkish tinge of her skin. With her hair arranged in loose waves around her face, she looked breathtakingly luminous, almost untouchable in her beauty.

"Alright, Castelo," he finally replied, trying to sound casual. "No need to threaten me with violence. I'll dance with you."

He hadn't really danced before, but he didn't care.

She didn't say anything when he took her hand. As they moved onto the dance floor in the middle of the auditorium, a slow ballad began to play. He put his hands on her waist; in response, she rested her hands lightly on his shoulders.

"Congratulations," he said as they began swaying to the music. "Heard your victory was a landslide."

She smiled up at him, the pride in her eyes unmistakable. "Thanks. Couldn't have done it without you."

His arms tightened around her, drawing her closer. He wondered if she noticed.

"Congratulations, too," she continued. "You had such a great game. No one could stop you out there. It was amazing to watch. I'm sure you'll go all the way to the championships again."

"Thanks," he replied, pulling her even closer until she was almost completely pressed against him. He wondered if she could feel the raging reaction of his body from being so close to hers. "Is this okay?"

She let out a nervous laugh but bobbed her head gently. "Is it just me or do I feel like we've done this before?"

"Maybe in another life," he answered, his lips brushing her hair.

She sighed and closed the last few inches that separated them, her arms coiling around his neck, as high and as tightly as her height would allow.

"What about this life?" she muttered against his chest. The warmth of her breath through the thin fabric of his shirt felt undeniably intimate.

"You tell me, Jeri."

"I don't know. Her cheek settled comfortably on the spot where his heart was. "But I don't want this to end."

She had no idea how much he'd wanted to say the exact same thing to her.

I wish my time with you would never end.

But the song was over, leaving him breathless and unsure of what to do next.

She stepped back, avoiding eye contact. He averted his eyes, too. Acknowledging the intensity of the moment might make it too real—once he crossed that line, there would be no turning back.

"Nick, can we talk about what just happened?" Her hand found his in the darkness. Her touch was cold and slightly damp. He knew his reaction was almost the same.

"Of course." It was all he could say.

She led him to a secluded corner at the backstage area of the auditorium, past layers upon layers of dusty dark red stage curtains, their way illuminated by a few old lightbulbs. Away from the crowd, they found themselves alone in what looked like a broken-down dressing room. There were two chairs in front of the cracked mirror. As if in silent agreement, they both stayed on their feet. She still clung to his hand, a little too tightly.

"I feel like I've taken advantage of our friendship and your kindness," she began hesitantly. "You've always been so nice to me and I feel like I've insulted you. I'm really sorry. I think I got carried away. Today has been particularly overwhelming."

Her voice was barely audible over the distant hum of

the ongoing party, but he could see the uncertainty and fear in her eyes in the semi-darkness.

What was she so afraid of?

He reached for her other hand, this time intertwining his fingers with hers. He brought her hands up to his chin, as if keeping them next to his skin would warm her up.

"You don't have to apologize. We danced. That was all, wasn't it?"

She shook her head. "Was it only a dance to you? I don't even know how to act around you anymore. I don't know what I feel for you. I don't even know what we have between us. It fucks with my head so badly."

Before she could say anything more, he leaned in and captured her lips in a kiss.

It was his first kiss.

And he let go.

It was passionate and intense. Again and again, their lips met, each kiss increasing in urgency with which he craved her touch, her taste.

"Is this the real you?" she whispered when they finally pulled apart, her breath ragged and her eyes wide with wonder.

"Yes," he responded without hesitation. "It is, only with you."

He didn't say anything more as his hands moved to

the straps of her dress, his fingertips brushing the softness of her skin as he slowly lowered the fabric to reveal more of her. He marveled at the curves and delicate lines of her body, everything that made her so perfect in his eyes.

"Nick, I..." she began to protest, stopping his hands in their path. "You know I'm not..." Her voice trailed off as she glanced down at herself.

"You're the most beautiful girl in the world to me, Jeri."

Tenderly, he explored her with his mouth. He started with her neck and chest, his tongue tracing circles around the taut nipples once her ample, perfectly round breasts found their way out of her bra. He settled her on the old dresser and kissed her lips before his fingers continued their journey downward.

"Trust me, you are perfect just as you are," he assured her, as he parted her legs, his hands tracing the curve of her hips before sliding her panties off.

He lifted the skirt of her dress and kissed his way from her knees upward, his tongue leaving a damp path along the way. His lips traced the curves of her inner thighs, inches away from the very heart of her that radiated white-hot heat. The scent of her engulfed him like an irresistibly intoxicating cloud; it was so uniquely her it was all he could do not to bury himself inside her.

He took a deep breath and pressed his lips to her

core, his tongue joyously lapping up the taste of her as she moaned and writhed on the dresser, her partially exposed breasts bouncing, her legs parting wider to make way for more of the sensations he was giving her.

"Nick," she panted, her hips grinding against his mouth. Her hands dug into his shoulders and pulled at his hair in turn as her movements increased in urgency. Jeri losing control against a broken dressing room mirror was the most incredibly erotic sight he had ever laid eyes on.

It took one more suckle at her nub and one more deep stroke of his fingers before she let out a loud moan, finally getting to the peak he so desperately wanted her to reach.

Her body stiffened, then abruptly went limp in the aftermath of her climax. He caught her in his arms as she wavered from her seated position. He held her close, listening to her rapid heartbeat, their breaths mingling together as the lingering scent of her engulfed his senses.

He savored the sensation of her legs wrapped loosely around his hips, her arms draped over his shoulders, her damp hair plastered all over her face and his. This was the most intimate he had ever been with anyone.

He was the first to speak, his lips against her ear as he inhaled her now-familiar cologne, mingled with her sweat, from the throbbing pulse on her neck. "I've never been with someone before. I've never even kissed anyone. You're the first."

"Me, too," she breathed. "You're my first kiss…the first boy who's ever touched me. You're my first everything."

She pulled him close, kissing his cheek and burying her nose in his hair. It was a strange, yet deeply moving, gesture.

"I've never had a boyfriend before," she continued. "I've always been so focused on my studies, on helping others, on being a student leader. I never had time for… love. Definitely not this kind."

"Until now?" He felt something akin to hope stir in his chest.

"Until now," she confirmed, almost shyly.

Their lips met again, tenderly at first, then more urgently, hungrily. His hands found her exposed breasts once more, but before he could reach for the damp spot between her legs again, her hands slid into his shirt.

She hesitated briefly before going lower, her fingers finally daring to reach inside his jeans. "Is this okay?"

"Y-yes," he stuttered as his body coiled in anticipation.

She reached into his underwear and took him in her hand. He gasped and cursed under his breath, gritting his teeth.

Encouraged, she continued, rubbing and stroking him.

He didn't know he could get any harder, but he did. He was almost at breaking point.

She slid off the dresser, straightening her clothes as she went, and pushed him against the wall. He was achingly aware she still wasn't wearing her panties; they were somewhere in a damp ball on one of the nearby chairs.

She went down on her knees and undid his zipper, pushing his underwear down just enough to free his rock-hard arousal. He groaned when she bent her head and took him into her mouth, her lips moving up and down his length in a maddening rhythm.

He felt an electric current shoot through him, and his entire body tensed as he climaxed right in her mouth. The waves of pleasure that coursed through his body were so strong they threatened to tear him apart. Her name escaped his lips in a raw, guttural moan, rumbling in his chest and through the dusty air of the backstage area.

She stood up and put her arms around his waist, as if to hold him upright.

"You're amazing," he whispered into her hair.

"So are you," she replied.

They kissed once more, tongues tangling, tasting each other with a newfound sense of closeness. He hardened again, almost immediately; this time, there was no hiding it from her.

"Jeri, what are we supposed to do now?"

"I don't know," she admitted, her fingers gripping his rumpled shirt tightly. "But I don't want us to end, whatever this is we've got."

I don't want us to end, he echoed inwardly.

They were an *'us'* now.

It was all he'd ever wanted.

Everything he'd ever needed, since the first time he saw her.

"Whatever you want to do, I'm here for you. I'll follow you anywhere."

"Would you?"

He nodded.

He felt, more than he saw, her smile.

He smiled back as his hand found hers in the shadows.

From then on, he never let go.

Act 2

Fallen

Six

The Desire

HE HAD HER IN HIS ARMS, FOR NOW.
As he held her, he still marveled at how they both appeared to be so different from each other.

She was the epitome of intelligence and charisma. Everyone liked her—from the teachers, to the cafeteria staff, most if not all of the student body. She always had that ready smile and the time to listen to everyone's problems.

People believed that sleeping wasn't on her busy schedule, the same way she believed he didn't sleep at all.

Everyone knew that Jeri Castelo would rather stay up talking to someone in her trademark high-octane and witty manner, organizing events as a member of the University Student Council for the second year in a row, or tutoring other students in Calculus.

He was popular in another fashion: the star football player who never gave away much about himself.

The name Aragon struck fear in the football teams of colleges all over the region. Ever since his freshman year, he had brought the university an unprecedented steady stream of championships.

He was not, however, raised to become an athletic achiever. His training had aimed to accomplish more serious ends.

Deadly serious ends.

In his first year, their class had gone on a trip up the mountains as part of their Biology subject. While everyone had lugged bags of canned goods and other packaged foods, he had only brought clothes and minimal camping equipment.

Evening at their campsite, the teacher had asked, "Where's the dinner you're supposed to bring for yourself?"

"It's right behind you, sir." He had thrown his hunting knife, the blade whizzing a mere inch above his professor's head.

A wild chicken, an *ilahas*, had squawked and crashed to the ground in rapid succession.

He then had an entire roasted chicken for his dinner, served hot. No one shared his meal, or spoke to him for the rest of the trip. The teacher gave him a grade of 1.0.

After that, everyone dealt with him very cautiously. No one dared to test his temper, even though he had never once displayed it, on or off the field.

He'd liked things that way, or so he thought. The further he distanced himself, the better.

Only Jeri had dared break through the wall between him and the rest of the world.

Ever since that fateful night more than a year ago, he knew he had fallen in love with her, more and more deeply with each passing day.

She had not been of any help, either. She had wanted and loved him, too.

At the end of the evening they first danced and kissed, they had made love, nervously and tenderly, on his tiny bed in the main building's basement.

He had never imagined he would feel that way, when his body, lean and hardened by years of training, was intertwined with hers, soft and welcoming.

He remembered the first time he'd touched her hair, the first time he'd allowed himself to look into her eyes without any qualms, the first time he'd kissed her as much as he wanted to.

He remembered the first time she'd allowed him to take off her clothes and taste all of her.

It was only later, in the aftermath of their passionate encounter, did he figure out that she'd reminded him of apples.

Since then, he had been unable to distance himself or stop thinking about her, no matter how hard he'd tried to deny how he really felt.

Ever since their freshman year, the distance between him and the perfection that was Jeri Castelo had seemed impossible to bridge.

She shone as brightly and as purely as the sun, on a day without clouds.

He was only a shadow, a dreary mass of dark secrets.

But, for now, he felt whole, from her touch and her light.

Now was all he ever had with her, he thought, as his reverie of their time together melted away, bringing him back into the present, with her in his bed, wrapped in his arms.

Jeri peeled off his shirt, her fingers brushing over the eagle tattoo etched over his heart. He felt her hands run over his shoulders and his stomach. With a moan, she moved closer, climbing onto his lap and wrapping her legs around his waist as they continued to kiss each other.

He reached up and began to unbutton her blouse, slowly revealing her delicate skin. His eyes drank in the sight of her, his heart racing with the familiar combination of desire and fear, as if he was seeing her for the first time all over again. He unclasped her bra and gently traced his fingers along her curves before lowering his mouth to her nipples, licking and biting them softly, making her gasp.

He continued to explore her body, his fingers deftly unzipping her skirt and slipping it off along with her panties until she was completely naked before him. Her pinkish skin was flushed under the lights.

He focused on her inner thighs, coaxing her to open for him, his body humming with excitement as she gave in so willingly and sweetly to his unspoken request. As his mouth descended upon her, she cried his name out, her hands pulling at his hair.

"Please don't stop, Nick." Her voice was barely audible above the pounding of his own heart, as his arousal tried to fight its way out of the confines of his clothes.

But he was going to take his time. Patience was something he was very good at.

He began tentatively, by tasting her, his tongue tracing intricate patterns across her sensitive flesh. His fingers soon joined the fray as he brought her to the peak, a hoarse scream coming from her throat.

He held her close as she slowly came down from the heights of her pleasure. He kissed her hair and her cheeks as she trembled in his arms, panting as if she had run around the campus herself.

He didn't have to wait very long for her to catch her breath.

She reached for the waistband of his joggers, slowly lowering them to reveal his hardness.

His gaze never left hers as he gently positioned himself between her legs. He took a moment to make sure she was wet, using his length to tease her entrance. The sensation of her slick folds against him always drove him to the very edge, no matter how many times he had her.

"Fuck, you feel so good."

She cupped his cheeks and kissed him soundly on the lips. "So do you."

With those words, she put her arms around his shoulders and her legs around his hips.

He allowed himself to sink deep into her. He wrapped his arms around her tightly as he began to thrust into her, slowly, languidly.

They began to move together in a sensual rhythm. He could feel the tension building within him, the heat and pressure coiling tighter and tighter as he lost himself in her embrace.

"I can't hold back," he gasped out as he teetered on the brink.

"Let go," she urged him softly. "I'm here with you. I love you."

With the warmth and tenderness of her reassurance enveloping him, he lost control, surrendering to the tidal wave of pleasure that crashed over him.

"I love you, too," he heard himself say. "Now come for me."

As he thrust into her in the final throes of his own climax, he heard her cry out his name as she, too, gave her surrender.

For now, she was with him, as close as two people could possibly be.

For now, her light was his, too.

Seven

The Dream

WAS THIS A DREAM?

His heart pounded as he gazed at the woman in his arms, their bodies tangled together on his narrow bed. His fingertips traced lazy patterns on her skin, marveling at the warmth of her that seemed to surround him completely.

When he finally found his voice, her name sounded like a desperate plea.

"Jeri."

She looked into his eyes, her own gaze reflecting his desire, before she cupped his cheek and leaned in to kiss him deeply. Their tongues danced together, exploring each other's mouths.

"Yes," she murmured between kisses. "Always yes."

With renewed vigor, he rolled them over, positioning himself above her once more. This time, she spread her legs wide, raising her hips to meet his mid-air. He slid his hands under her buttocks to lift her slightly, and then filled her in one quick surge.

He reveled in the sensation of her body fitting so perfectly against his, in the way she responded to his touch—and he to hers. He came with a thunderous roar, as she shook under him, her hair spreading all over his pillow as her breasts bounced enticingly with each of thrust.

It wasn't too long before he took her again, this time from behind, his hands gripping her hips tightly before moving to cup her breasts and caress her nipples.

After they recovered, he held her in his lap, their faces close as if sharing the same breath, as they exchanged tender kisses while they made love once more.

He didn't care if this was all only a dream.

It was a heady blend of tender emotion and fiery passion. He knew he would never tire of the feel of her body against his, the way her moans and sighs echoed in his ears, the softness of her arms around him.

He was completely and utterly lost in her.

Momentarily sated, they lay quietly in each other's arms.

"You should eat more," she declared out of the blue. "I need to bring you more food."

"Really?"

"Yes. I don't know where you get all that energy to move so fast, or kick that hard. Or to run so much every day." Her breath tickled the bare skin of his chest. "Or to do *this*."

"I don't know. Habit, maybe."

They both lapsed into silence.

She reached for his hands. He felt her delicate skin brush against his scarred and calloused palms.

"It must be time for practice soon," she finally said.

He found his phone in the pocket of his discarded joggers. The display told him they still had a little more than an hour left before he had to go to the field.

He turned to look at her, naked in his bed, his blanket wrapped around her for modesty. "Would you like some breakfast?"

She nodded. "I'm starving."

He put his phone away and joined her, reaching for her underneath the blanket.

"Me, too."

As he took her back into his arms and kissed her again, he hoped he could stay in the dream long enough.

Eight

The Deception

THE SKY WAS STILL A DEEP, MURKY GREY WHEN they walked out of the main building. Morning, classes, and the rest of the world would be upon them soon.

She paused when they reached the middle of the quad, her eyes settling on the grassy field in front of them.

"The first time I saw you, you were practicing alone," she said softly. "It was the first day of freshman year. It was Orientation Week and I came in early. I wanted to introduce myself to people as they arrived. I saw you on the field when I walked up to this spot, right here."

He swallowed hard as he absorbed the weight of her

words, the depth of the memory she now shared. All he could do was take her hand and listen.

"It was like watching something both magnificent and deadly at the same time. It was raining, but you never even missed a shot. The way you moved, the way you stood there, on your own, defying the downpour…you didn't seem to care. You were just so focused and determined. But I never approached you because I thought… well, I thought you'd only be interested in tall, pretty girls, like the ones football players and jocks usually go for."

He felt a chuckle rumble through his chest.

Very few people had seen him smile. But she was the only one who heard him laugh.

She elbowed him in the ribs "What the hell's so funny?"

"You." He pulled her close as they looked at the field still blanketed by darkness. "Why do you always have to be so fucking *perfect*? You remember, know, and do almost everything."

Her breathing seemed to stop. It took moments before she could answer. "I was raised to be like that. No one could make up for my mistakes, if I was stupid enough to make them. When I moved in with my grandparents after my parents died, I learned this very quickly."

She paused, as if gathering momentum. "When I was

little, my grandmother would slap my hands with a stick whenever I couldn't spell a word correctly. Or, sometimes, they wouldn't let me have dinner unless I could recite an entire speech without any mistakes. I got good at all of it. Then better. By the time I was eight, there was no more need for such discipline. I delivered everything they wanted."

"When I got older, my grandparents told me my mother failed them by eloping with my father. She had me when she was eighteen. And I…I couldn't fail my family."

The words had a pained, bitter edge. He could taste them in his own heart. If there was someone who understood, only too well, how it was like to rise to the nearly impossible expectations and demands of their family, it was him.

"It gets exhausting. I'm doing a great job at it, though. There are so many people expecting so many things. I had to do all those things. I feel guilty when I couldn't. Sometimes it's like digging your own grave. But you need to do it anyway." Her voice sounded rough and strained. "Being perfect was the only way to survive, to keep having value."

The first few raindrops fell. He felt them on his arm.

Then he realized they weren't from the sky. The droplets were her tears.

Something bubbled inside him. It wasn't rage, but a calmer desire to kill. It was part of him, his lifeblood.

Although he had vowed to himself never to take a human life again, he would break that for her, to spare her from any further pain.

But there was no one entirely responsible for the sort of torment she felt. Just like no one had to pay for his past and the choices he'd made, except perhaps he himself.

"I'm sorry…" His voice trailed off. He felt lame and helpless, as the familiar cold numbness ran the length of his spine. It was a feeling only pulling the trigger could relieve. "I shouldn't have said–"

"It's not your fault. Sometimes I just couldn't help but think about this, no matter how hard I try not to." She bravely swallowed back her sobs as he wiped her tears away. "I had it coming. I had it coming all these years. It was only a matter of time before I got burned out."

He waited for her to calm down. She could so easily collect herself, or at least appear to have done so. He was the only one who would always know and feel the trembling of her hands, the uneven beating of her pulse, even if she appeared perfectly composed.

She had looked like this during debates when she ran

for the University Student Council a second time, when after she'd felt like ice to his touch. Everyone else had praised her composure and quick thinking, never considering the amount of control it took on her part.

With all the light she radiated, she still had the cold, dark parts, too.

Nine

The Deal

"I was raised to be the best, too," he admitted, slowly, cautiously. "I became the best."

Jeri's tearstained face had a look that showed the struggle to comprehend his words. She said nothing, but spoke volumes with wide eyes.

He knew at that point he had to explain, to make her understand.

There was no turning back now, not after everything they had shared.

"When I was in high school, I was known as Cain in the underground. My father chose that name for me. I was born with a twin brother, but my cord was around his neck when we were cut out…I choked him to death in our mother's womb."

"I didn't know…" She was grasping at words. "You never—"

He squeezed her hands in his, shaking his head slightly.

It was his way of telling her it was okay. He would be okay, if he had her with him.

"I'm the youngest of five brothers, but I could outshoot all of them. I could take them all down hand to hand, too, by the time I was seven. I was faster and stronger. I was even better in most sports. A lot of schools offered everything from bribes to scholarship packages to my parents so I would go to their place, just so they could get all the football titles, even a National Games medal."

"My father told us that the mantle of the Eagle-Eye had to be passed down. He was almost sixty and it was about time for him to mentor the next one. All my uncles—everyone in my family—wanted me to take it. I was fourteen. The Eagle-Eye tattoo meant the world."

"That explains the eagle mark on your chest." Jeri placed her hand over his heart. "It's more than just a tattoo."

"Our family has been in the Philippines for more than three hundred years. You can say we wrote a lot of history in blood and no one ever knew. We are loyal to no one, except our own kin and land. That's how we had roots. The

Eagle-Eye is the best of the present generation. He was entrusted to carry out the most dangerous missions."

He said everything without any pride. Then again, there was nothing to be proud of.

A series of frozen frames flashed in his memory. He drew in a sharp breath at how vividly he could remember the events of seven years past.

"My initiation rite was to kill a priest who had sexually abused the son of one of our workers at the corn farm. The boy was eight, a *sacristan*. It was three-thirty in the morning…the priest was walking to Church to prepare for the *misa de gallo*. I got him with one shot, right between the eyes. It was Christmas—and my fifteenth birthday—when I became the ninth-generation Eagle-Eye. That's when I got the tattoo. Then my father said, 'You will be Cain now.'"

"There are twenty-nine others on my list; two of them were very young, maybe seven or eight years old. They were the children of a drug lord who thought he could smuggle *shabu* through one of the canning companies in our town. They saw me shoot their father. *Leave no witnesses*. That was in the rules."

"You killed people." Her voice was toneless. Not angry, afraid or accusing, just clear and audible.

"I left Surallah thinking I could somehow lose that part of me. I bargained for four years to finish college so there's time to think about it. No matter how hard you try, that side of you stays right where it is. If you try to get rid of it somehow, it will eat you up alive. You could shed your skin, but not your blood. You wouldn't have the strength to survive."

He realized she had not backed away, or showed any sign of fear or disgust.

Before he could say anything more, she looked straight into his eyes, unblinking. He could see the clarity in her gaze, behind the sheen of tears, in the soft light of the oncoming sunrise.

"I love you, Nick. Nothing's going to change that."

Ten

The Dawn

NICK.

He was only ever Aragon to everyone else. To Jeri, he'd always been her Nick.

The absence of revulsion from her took him aback. "I know I should have told you before. I couldn't, Jeri. I didn't want to lose you. I'm so sorry—"

"There's nothing to be sorry for." Her tone was firm, although she spoke in a voice so quiet it was almost carried away by the early morning breeze. "I loved you for what you are. I found in you a part of myself I thought I'd never find in anyone else."

He swallowed hard, ice and dread gripping his insides. "You're not angry, are you?"

She shook her head. "Why should I be? Because you told me the truth?"

"But I'm a…*killer*. You should be walking away right now."

Jeri did the exact opposite.

She put her arms around him. "I'm staying right here. I'm not going anywhere. Don't you know how good it feels to finally hear you talk about where you came from?"

"Jeri, I…" His voice trailed off. He had no words for her. He only had himself and everything else. He'd lay them all at her feet in a heartbeat.

She took his hand and placed it gently on her belly. "I love you for being the father of this child."

It took him a second to understand what she meant by both her actions and words. When he finally did, he felt all the air leave his lungs.

He could only stare at her as a sudden glow began to form in the pit of his stomach. It was the familiar warmth he had known only when he met her.

When he finally mustered some semblance of self-control, he said, "Are you…?"

He couldn't finish the question. The idea was too

unreal, too beautiful, to speak of. Part of him feared it would disappear right before his eyes, along with her.

Instead, she smiled brightly. "Maybe six weeks now. A doctor who doesn't know my family confirmed it yesterday afternoon. That's why I had to see you. I could no longer keep this a secret." Her face, so breathtakingly beautiful to him, was a study in mixed emotions. "I had to tell you."

"I'm going to be a father," he said slowly, tasting the word. He put his hands on her stomach, over her own. His own blood, now with hers.

Father, he repeated inwardly. A father.

She nodded.

This time, the first real drops of rain started to fall.

A droplet landed on his lips. He tasted sweetness and warmth. It bore none of the bitter taste and spilled blood of the past three hundred years.

A bolt of lightning streaked across the sky, followed by a loud rumble of thunder, just before the rain came down in earnest.

In silent agreement, neither of them suggested taking shelter in the nearby gazebos surrounding the campus quad.

Jeri stepped back and spread out her arms, giggling as she turned her face up to the downpour.

As he watched her spinning slowly under the rain, he realized that he was still half-stunned by her news.

She paused for a moment, her movements punctuated by a soft giggle. "Nick, I want to dance with you."

In that moment, his head cleared, as if someone had shone a light on the shadows of his burden. He took her hands in his and placed her palms over his heart, on the very same spot where his body bore the Eagle-Eye mark. "I love you."

She smiled and stood on tiptoe, pressing her lips to his. "For the first time in our lives, let's not be the best assassin or the perfect girl. Let's do the right thing and just be us."

He nodded. "Us," he repeated, trying the sound of the word rolling off his tongue.

He'd always liked the ring of it, remembering the first time she had used the word to describe what they had.

I don't want us to end.

The rain fell harder.

He basked in the sight of the woman who had looked him in the eye and never wavered, even after his confession and the deaths he had brought.

Instead, she embraced him and his blood.

She looked straight back at him, the same way she had the night of their first dance. The night she'd opened the door to his heart and, unwittingly, to his freedom from the shadows of the past.

Nicholas Aragon embraced her then.

Nothing more was said.

The rain crashed around them, drenching concrete, earth, steel, and their bodies.

When the sun finally rose, the thunderstorm came to an end. Only the wind was left howling, singing a dirge to the shadows as they became one with the light.

Epilogue

The Last Letter

It was Lexie's habit, for the past two years now, to drop by the newspaper office every morning to check on messages and writing assignments.

When she arrived, on the dot, at half-past seven, the first thing she noticed was a folded note tacked to the corkboard. Her name was on it, in a familiar roundish script.

She took the paper off the board and unlocked the door.

The note felt slightly damp in her hands as she unfolded it. The paper seemed to have gotten wet in the heavy rain earlier that morning and was slowly drying out.

> My dearest Lexie,
> 　I've held on for years to what I thought I was.
> 　I have become the perfect puppet to expectations that were never mine. It's time to cut the strings.
> 　I gave them my entire life, until now. From today, it's my turn to live the rest of it on my own terms.
> 　I will miss you.
> Love always,
> Jeri

She stared at the signature. Like her best friend's personality, it had an undeniable, inimitable flourish.

For a long time, Lexie stood in the middle of the empty office, her gaze seeing beyond the unlit space before her.

She went through the drafts left on the table for her to review, locked up, and headed to her first class of the day.

Along the way, she stopped by one of the trash cans on the quad and tore the letter to shreds. She watched the tiny white pieces fall from her hands like raindrops disappearing into the cold morning air.

"Be happy, Jeri," she whispered. "I'll miss you, too."

About the Author

Shirley Siaton writes edgy and evocative stories and poems. Her worlds are in a deliciously dark cross-section of the romance, neo-noir, action, fantasy, new adult, and contemporary genres.

She has several books of fiction and poetry released since February 2023. Her first book is the free verse collection *Black Cat and other poems*. She also pens juvenile literature as Shirley Parabia.

She is an award-winning writer, poet and journalist in English, Filipino and Hiligaynon, lauded by the Stevan Javellana Foundation, Philippine Information Agency, and West Visayas State University. Her essays, short stories, and poems have been published internationally in print and digital media. Her multi-lingual plays have been staged in the Philippines.

Shirley is a black belt in Shotokan Karate and an international certified fitness coach. Originally from Iloilo City, she is based in the Middle East with her husband and two daughters.

On the Web

Shirley's official website:
shirleysiaton.com

Complete reading guide:
shirley.pub

Subscribe to Shirley's VIP list for free exclusive updates:
newsletter.shirleysiaton.com

www.ingramcontent.com/pod-product-compliance
Lightning Source LLC
LaVergne TN
LVHW040105080526
838202LV00045B/3781